Kobee Manatee™

A Wild Weather Adventure

Written by **Robert Scott Thayer**

Illustrated by **Lauren Gallegos**

Thompson Mill Press

For Jillaine
-R.S.T.

For Kirsti and her little ones
-L.G.

Visit Kobee Manatee™ on the Web!
KobeeManatee.com

Many thanks go out to all who helped in the making of this book, in particular; Susan Korman, editor and Rob Marciano, ABC News Senior Meteorologist.

Published by Thompson Mill Press LLC
2865 South Eagle Road, #368
Newtown, Pennsylvania 18940
thompsonmillpress.com

Library of Congress Cataloging in Publication Data
Thayer, Robert Scott.
Kobee manatee: a wild weather adventure / written by Robert Scott Thayer; illustrated by Lauren Gallegos. – 1st ed.
p. cm.

Summary: Kobee Manatee travels from Key West, Florida to Nassau, in the Bahamas so he can surprise his sister Kim on her birthday, but runs into wild weather as he crosses the mighty Atlantic Ocean.

ISBN 978-0-9883269-4-1 (hardcover)   2014949235

Printed and Bound in the USA

The illustrations were created with acrylic on illustration board.
First edition, first printing
Designed by Lauren Gallegos

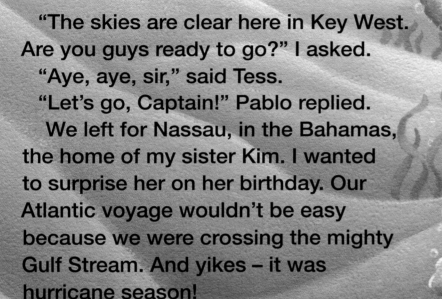

"The skies are clear here in Key West. Are you guys ready to go?" I asked.

"Aye, aye, sir," said Tess.

"Let's go, Captain!" Pablo replied.

We left for Nassau, in the Bahamas, the home of my sister Kim. I wanted to surprise her on her birthday. Our Atlantic voyage wouldn't be easy because we were crossing the mighty Gulf Stream. And yikes – it was hurricane season!

Kobee's Fun Facts

The Atlantic Hurricane season in the Northern Hemisphere starts on June 1st and runs through November 30th. A tropical storm needs to have winds of at least 74 miles per hour to become a hurricane. The Saffir-Simpson Wind Scale classifies hurricanes:

Category 1: *74 - 95 mph*

Category 2: *96 - 110 mph*

Category 3: *111 - 129 mph*

Category 4: *130 - 156 mph*

Category 5: *157 mph or higher*

"How far away is Nassau?" Tess asked.

"About three hundred miles," I said.

"That's pretty far away," said Pablo.

"How long will it take you to swim there?" Tess asked.

"Well … moving at five miles per hour with some stops, about three days," I replied.

"Look!" Pablo called, "White wispy clouds!"

"They're cirrus," I said.

Tess looked around in surprise. "What circus?" she asked.

"No," I chuckled. "*Cirrus* – they're cirrus clouds."

"Oh … They look like thin, swirly strings," Tess answered.

We zoomed past Key Largo.

Kobee's Fun Facts

Cirrus \'sir-əs\ clouds are thin, feathery clouds. They're made of ice crystals and are found at heights above 20,000 feet. These clouds signal that a change in the weather is on the way.

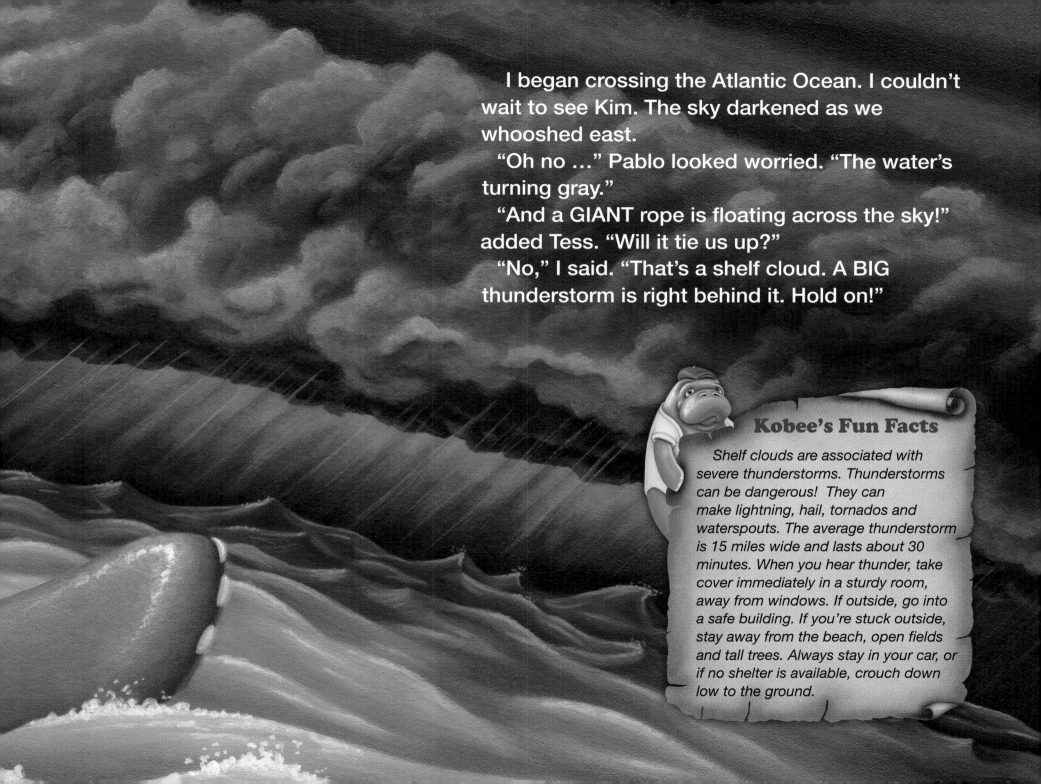

I began crossing the Atlantic Ocean. I couldn't wait to see Kim. The sky darkened as we whooshed east.

"Oh no ..." Pablo looked worried. "The water's turning gray."

"And a GIANT rope is floating across the sky!" added Tess. "Will it tie us up?"

"No," I said. "That's a shelf cloud. A BIG thunderstorm is right behind it. Hold on!"

Kobee's Fun Facts

Shelf clouds are associated with severe thunderstorms. Thunderstorms can be dangerous! They can make lightning, hail, tornados and waterspouts. The average thunderstorm is 15 miles wide and lasts about 30 minutes. When you hear thunder, take cover immediately in a sturdy room, away from windows. If outside, go into a safe building. If you're stuck outside, stay away from the beach, open fields and tall trees. Always stay in your car, or if no shelter is available, crouch down low to the ground.

Two lightning bolts shot right past us. The sky rumbled and roared. Suddenly something threw Tess and Pablo into the raging sea. "It's a waterspout!" I shouted as it pulled me into the air!

"Kobee, come back!" screamed Tess.
Pablo looked determined. "We'll save you, Kobee!"

My purple cap flew off as I spun higher ... and higher ...and h i g h e r.

Kobee's Fun Facts

There are two types of waterspouts: tornadic and fair weather. Tornadic waterspouts are tornados that form over water, or tornados that move from land to water. They are linked to severe thunderstorms. Fair weather waterspouts form at the flat bases of developing cumulus clouds. This type of waterspout is not associated with thunderstorms.

As the funnel fizzled out, I **S P L A S H E D** into the water.

Kobee's Fun Facts

Lightning causes thunder. Its temperature is about 54,000 degrees Fahrenheit. Cloud-to-ground lightning bolts hit Earth 100 times per second! Each bolt can hold up to 1 billion volts of electricity. Lightning also can strike from 10 or more miles away. So take cover inside until all thunder sounds are gone, even if the sun comes out!

"Kobee, are you okay?" Tess asked.
"I'm d-i-z-z-y," I said.
"Whew." Pablo looked relieved. "That was scary," he said. "Kobee, here's your cap."
"Thanks," I replied. "Wind is powerful!"

The storm passed.

"Wow … Creamy cotton clouds," Tess said.

"What kind are they?" she asked.

"Cumulus clouds," I replied.

"Hey!" Pablo grinned. "That cloud looks like you, Kobee!"

Kobee's Fun Facts

Cumulus clouds are fair weather clouds. Their bases are flat and they're not very tall. You see them when the sky is blue. If the tops of these clouds start growing into a cauliflower-shaped tower, they become known as Cumulus congestus clouds, with all kinds of shapes and characters in them!

Cumulonimbus clouds are dark thunderstorm clouds. Thunderstorms are caused by warm unstable air, moisture, and lift. The lift is created by fronts, sea breezes, mountains, or just the sun heating the ground on a hot summer day.

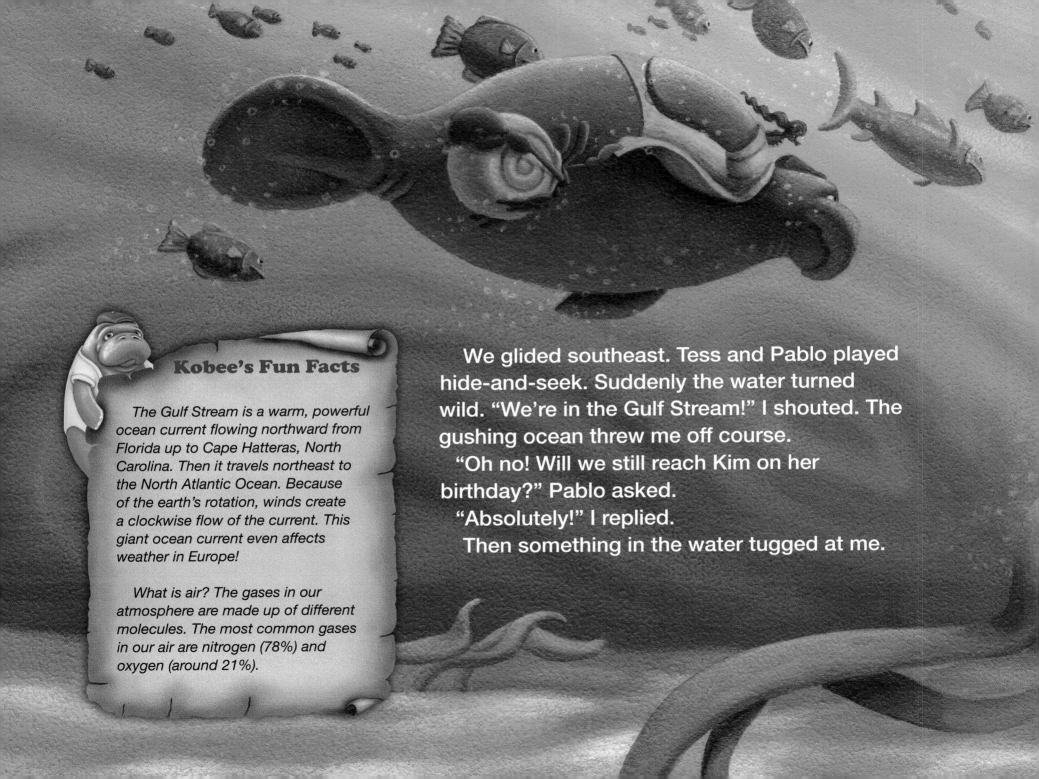

Kobee's Fun Facts

The Gulf Stream is a warm, powerful ocean current flowing northward from Florida up to Cape Hatteras, North Carolina. Then it travels northeast to the North Atlantic Ocean. Because of the earth's rotation, winds create a clockwise flow of the current. This giant ocean current even affects weather in Europe!

What is air? The gases in our atmosphere are made up of different molecules. The most common gases in our air are nitrogen (78%) and oxygen (around 21%).

We glided southeast. Tess and Pablo played hide-and-seek. Suddenly the water turned wild. "We're in the Gulf Stream!" I shouted. The gushing ocean threw me off course.

"Oh no! Will we still reach Kim on her birthday?" Pablo asked.

"Absolutely!" I replied.

Then something in the water tugged at me.

"A rip current!" I called.
"It's got Tess," screamed Pablo.
"Don't panic, Tess!" I yelled.

Kobee's Fun Facts

A rip current is a very strong current that flows away from the shore. It is usually narrow in width. If you get caught in one, don't panic. Swim parallel to shore, and then swim back in.

"Great job, Tess," Pablo said. "I would have panicked in the rip current."
"I was really scared," Tess admitted. "But I just floated, and then swam out of the current when I could."

"What are those white scaly clouds?" Tess asked me.

"Cirrocumulus," I said. "Yikes … They can bring dangerous weather."

"Did you say dangerous weather, Kobee?" asked Pablo.

"Yep." I swam faster. Trouble was ahead.

"Why are the clouds spinning backwards?" Tess asked.

"Because they're the outer bands of a hurricane," I replied.

Pablo's eyes went wide. "Eek! A hurricane?"

I nodded. "We're heading right into it!"

The east winds swirled. The raging water grabbed my flippers. I went for air just as a GIANT wave spun us around like a washing machine.

Kobee's Fun Facts

Cirrocumulus clouds look like fish scales and are sometimes called a "mackerel sky." These high clouds usually are seen with cirrus clouds. In winter, cirrocumulus predict fair, cold, weather.

Then the sun appeared. Everything got quiet.

"The hurricane is over!" cheered Pablo.

"No," I told my friends. "It's not over. We're in the hurricane's eye!"

"Can it see us?" Tess asked.

"No," I said. "The eye is the storm's center. That means the other half is still coming!"

Kobee's Fun Facts

Did you know that an average hurricane is about 300 miles wide? The eye of a hurricane is between 20 to 40 miles wide. During the eye, the air is calm and the sun can even come out! Don't let that fool you. Once the eye passes, the final part of the hurricane arrives, and it can be even stronger then the first part of the storm!

One of the largest hurricane waves ever recorded was 91 feet tall. It was created on September 15, 2004, by Hurricane Ivan in the Gulf of Mexico.

The wind went wild again. This time it came from the west.

"Hold on," I shouted as my strength came back.

"Oh no!" Pablo looked terrified. "The whole sky's spinning!"

Kobee's Fun Facts

Hurricane winds change direction after its center (eye) passes. In the Northern Hemisphere, storms rotate counterclockwise. In the Southern Hemisphere, storms rotate clockwise. These circular motions are caused by the Coriolis Effect. The Coriolis Effect is caused by the earth's rotation.

"Look. Those clouds just turned north," I said. "The hurricane is leaving!"

The sun came out and I saw something huge ahead.

"Paradise Island!" I said happily. "We're near Nassau."

"Whew!" Pablo said.

"Kim swims along these beaches," I said. We passed beautiful coral reefs and all kinds of fish. Then I saw something BIG!

Kobee's Fun Facts

What's the temperature? The United States uses the English or Fahrenheit measurement for temperature. However, the majority of the world uses the metric or Celsius measurement. For example, if it were 68 degrees Fahrenheit in Philadelphia, U.S.A., it would be 20 degrees Celsius in Toronto, Canada!

Did you know a raindrop falls at an average speed of 17 miles per hour?

It was a manatee, "Kim!" I shouted. "Happy Birthday!"

"Kobee! What a surprise little brother!" Kim said.

"Sis, I have music for your party!" I replied.

"Great! My birthday party is at Blue Lagoon Island," said Kim.

"Awesome!" Tess and Pablo replied.

"Kobee, I want to show you something on our way to Blue Lagoon!" Kim said.

"Great!" I replied.

In the distance I saw a GIANT underwater jungle.

"Seagrass Heaven!" Kim shouted.

"It's so green!" Pablo said.

"Blue Lagoon is straight ahead," said Kim.

Kobee's Fun Facts

Tornadoes are most frequent in the United States, where they occur about a 1000 times per year. Tornado Alley, in the south-central U.S., has the most tornadoes. Forecasters use the Enhanced Fujita Scale to record tornado wind speeds:

EF 0: 65 - 85 miles per hour (mph)

EF 1: 86 - 110 mph

EF 2: 111 - 135 mph

EF 3: 136 - 165 mph

EF 4: 166 - 200 mph

EF 5: Winds over 200 mph

Kobee's Fun Facts

Did you know that fog is a cloud at ground level?

Did you know our sky is blue because of the way the light scatters and moves through the atmosphere?

"Look! Stingrays!" Pablo said.

"They love it here," Kim said.

"Warm clear water, manatees love it too," I chuckled.

"We're at Blue Lagoon!" Kim shouted.

"Wow, look at all of Kim's friends!" Tess said.

Pablo grinned. "I see a GIANT seagrass birthday cake!"

I grabbed a guitar and sang, "Happy Birthday, Sis!" Then I strummed a tune about our wild weather adventure!

HAPPY BIRTHDAY KIM

Kobee's Fun Facts

Did you know the study of weather is called meteorology?